The Dancing Stones

by

Maggie Pearson

Illustrated by Peter Clover

To Melissa Davis, Emily Spence and
Sophia Cole, with thanks for their help.

First published in 2010 in Great Britain by
Barrington Stoke Ltd
18 Walker St, Edinburgh, EH3 7LP

www.barringtonstoke.co.uk

Copyright © 2010 Maggie Pearson
Illustrations © Peter Clover

ISBN: 978-1-84299-755-0

Printed in Great Britain by Bell & Bain Ltd

Contents

Chapter 1
Stones Can't Dance

The dancing stones. That's what Nan called them.

"But stones can't dance," said Kelly.

She's my sister.

"Stones can't dance," she said.

I'm Ben, by the way. Ben and Kelly. We sound like a brand of ice cream. What was Mum thinking about when she picked our names?

What was she thinking about when she booked that holiday in Spain?

Spain for Easter! Sun, sea and sand! Magic!

The bad news was Mum had only booked two tickets. She was going with Bob, who looks like a walrus. Sad eyes, no chin and a droopy moustache.

Kelly and me were off to Nan's for the
week. "It will give her a chance to get to
know you better," said Mum.

Lucky Nan. Not.

"You know I've only got two bedrooms
now?" said Nan.

"Ben and Kelly can share," said Mum.

"I'm not sharing with him!" said Kelly.

"Why not?" I said.

"Why not?" said Mum.

Kelly rolled her eyes. "I'm 14, Mum! And he's a boy."

"He's your brother," said Mum. "You can share a room with your brother."

"He farts in bed," said Kelly.

"You snore," I said.

"You see what they're like, Nan?" said
Mum. "I need a break."

"I'll sleep on the sofa," said Nan. "Then
they can each have their own room."

"That's sorted then," said Mum.

Nan used to live in a big, old house in town. Now she's got this little bungalow in the country.

"No more stairs!" said Nan. "And only a small garden to look after! I hate gardening."

She gets old Mr Frost to come in and do a bit of gardening for her.

"Call me Jack," he said. He smiled,
showing his gums. No teeth. Just gums.

Kelly looked away. She pointed up at the
hill. "What are those stones up there, Nan?"
she said.

Nan said, "They're the Dancing Stones."

Kelly said, "Stones can't dance."

Mr Frost took off his cap and rubbed his bald head. "They weren't always stones," he said.

"What do you mean, not always stones?" I said.

Kelly rolled her eyes. "OK. We give up. What were they before they were stones?"

Mr Frost put his cap back on and chewed his gums for a bit. "People," he said.

"People?" said Kelly. "People who were turned to stone?"

"Like fossils?" I asked. "Dinosaurs and stuff like that?"

"Not fossils." Mr Frost shook his head. "They're not as old as fossils."

"So how did they turn to stone?" I said.

"Don't ask me how," he said. "Ask me why."

"Why, then?" said Kelly.

"For dancing on a Sunday. They were called The Merry Dancers. That's the stones' other name. Not so merry now, eh?" He smiled, showing his toothless gums again.

Kelly looked as if she might be sick.

"Let's walk up there and have a look at them," said Nan.

"Let's not," said Kelly.

"You coming, Ben?" said Nan.

"OK," I said.

Chapter 2
Dancing on Sunday

They were just a bunch of big stones, after all. Twelve of them, as tall as people, standing in a circle. So what was all the fuss about?

They were stones. They had always been stones.

Then I touched one.

And it was warm.

I patted it. It was rough, like Dad's chin when he forgot to shave.

I took a step back and looked up at it.

And it was as if that stone was looking
back. Winking at me over its shoulder.

I took out the camera Dad gave me last birthday. (Must have cost him a shed-load of money.) I wanted to catch that winking look.

I went on taking pictures of the stones till Nan said it was time to go back.

"So what's the story, Nan?" said Kelly, while we were sat having our tea. "What were those people doing dancing up there, anyway? Why were they there?"

"Why not?" said Nan. And she told us the story. "It was a fine Saturday night. A full moon. And a fiddler was playing for them. Then, just before midnight, the fiddler stopped playing. 'I'm not playing on a Sunday,' he said. 'Not for dancing.' Off he went, home to his bed and to church the next morning. They all stopped dancing and they thought the party was over. Then they heard the sound of another fiddle. One by one, they began to dance again. Once they'd begun, they found they couldn't stop. Not till the church clock struck midnight."

"That's when they turned to stone?" I said.

"When the last stroke of midnight struck." Nan nodded. "And it was Sunday morning."

"But what's wrong with dancing on a Sunday?" said Kelly.

"When I was your age," said Nan, "Sundays were a day off work so you could go to church. There were no shops open on Sundays. No sport. No kids playing in the street."

"And no dancing?" I said.

"That's right," said Nan.

"Why did you put up with it?" said Kelly.

Nan gave a shrug. "It was just the way things were. I wasn't afraid of being turned to stone! But that's a very old story. Hundreds of years ago maybe there were people who really did think that way."

"Weird!" said Kelly.

That night I looked out of my bedroom window at the circle of stones on the hill.

I got the odd feeling that the stones were looking back at me.

I drew the curtains, climbed back into bed and hid myself deep down under the duvet.

I said to Mr Frost next day, "Do you ever get the feeling the stones are watching you?"

"Not much else for them to do, is there?" he said. "Only watch and wait."

"What do you think they're waiting for?"
I asked.

"They're waiting to dance again."

"But they'd have to turn back into people first," I said.

"Wouldn't it be great if they did dance again?" said Kelly, when I told her what Mr Frost had said. "Wouldn't it be great, Nan, if you could bring the stones back to life?"

"Would it?" said Nan. "Think about it. How long do you think they've been standing out there in all weathers? Sun, frost, wind and rain. What does the weather do to stone?"

"It wears it away," I said. "We did that in geography."

"So how do you think they'd look now," said Nan, "if they did come back to life?"

I thought about it. I thought of the stone that seemed to wink at me. It only seemed to wink because it had only got one eye. No nose, no ears, no hair, no mouth. Just one eye.

"They wouldn't be human any more," I said. "They'd be monsters."

"And how do you think they'd feel?" said Nan.

I knew how I'd feel. I'd be angry!

Chapter 3
Up to Something

Kelly can't live, she says, without her friends around her. The good news is it takes her about five minutes to find a whole bunch of new friends.

Me, I couldn't see the point in making friends. We were only staying with Nan for

23

a week. I was busy trying out my new camera anyway.

I thought Kelly might like a few photos to remember her new friends by.

The girls were hanging out by the church-yard wall. I crept through the grave-yard, using the wall for cover. I hoped they wouldn't see me but they did.

I heard Kelly say, "Take no notice. He's just my little brother."

They went on chatting.

I didn't think I was doing anything wrong. I thought she wanted me to take some photos of them, right?

No one was more shocked than me when one of them yelled, "He's got a camera!"

She shouted so loud it nearly split my ear-drums.

Then panic broke loose. Ooh! Shock horror! Like they were a bunch of D-list celebs and I was going to get their picture in the papers.

"Were you taking pictures of us?" said Kelly.

"No," I said. "OK. Yes. Maybe. What if I was?"

"Give me that!" She held out her hand for the camera.

"No way!" I said. And I nipped off as fast as I could, zig-zagging among the grave-stones, and legged it back to Nan's.

"Were you spying on us?" said Kelly while we were waiting for our take-away curry to come that evening.

"Spying on you?" I said. "When?"

"This afternoon. By the church-yard wall. Were you listening to what we were saying?"

"No," I said. "Why?"

"No reason," said Kelly.

She was up to something. I can always tell.

I said to Mr Frost next day, "Kelly's up to something."

"Oh, yes," he said. "She's up to something." He looked up at the circle of stones on the hill. "Kelly and her friends don't believe the story," he said.

"About the stones, you mean?" I said. "But it is just a story, isn't it? Do you believe it?"

He chewed his gums for a bit. Then he said, "I believe it's better to be safe than sorry. Some people just have to learn the hard way."

He picked up his spade and started digging again. Nan said he was making a trench for runner beans. It looked to me more spooky than that. It was more like he was digging a grave.

I'd be glad when this holiday was over.

Chapter 4
The Party

Saturday evening, before I went to bed, I packed my bag, ready for Mum and Bob to collect us on Sunday.

I couldn't sleep.

I couldn't see my watch in the dark, so I got up and went to the window. My watch said ten o'clock.

Then I heard Kelly's window open. I saw her climbing out.

I opened my window. "Where are you going?" I said softly.

I saw she was carrying her iPod speaker unit. The one Dad gave her for her birthday.

"Is it a party?" I said. "Can I come?"

Kelly said, "Sorry. Girls only."

Someone had lit a bonfire up on the hill.
I saw flames leaping up and shadows moving
among the stones.

I said, "Mr Frost said you were up to something."

"He tried to frighten us off," said Kelly. "He said if the twelve of us dance up there till after midnight the twelve stones will come to life again. Whoo! Scary, yeah? Here's the best bit!" Kelly laughed. "We'll all be turned to stone in their place! Don't look so worried, Ben. It's just a story."

A story. That's all it was. That's what I told myself, anyway. But it was cold and dark. The only noise was the wind sighing in the trees, blowing clouds across the moon, scattering the shadows.

Kelly was a pain.

But she was my sister.

Nothing would happen to her up there, would it?

What would I tell Mum if it did?

It took me just a few minutes to put some clothes on and find my shoes. I

climbed out of my window and followed
Kelly up the hill.

Music was playing now from Kelly's iPod
speaker. Girls were dancing, giggling,
chatting, passing round nibbles and cans of
Coke, whatever.

"Kelly!" I said softly.

"Go away!" she said. "It's just a party. You're not invited. So back off!"

I backed off.

Back down the hill and into the trees, where I tripped over something in the dark.

Another stone.

Number thirteen.

Twelve dancers – and me. Number thirteen.

That's when I knew I had to do something. I had to stop the girls dancing after midnight. Like Mr Frost said, it's better to be safe than sorry. And his story might just be true.

Chapter 5
Midnight

I crept back up the hill, keeping to the shadows, using the standing stones for cover. All I had to do was stop them dancing. Stop the music before midnight struck.

I grabbed the iPod speaker unit, feeling for the off-switch as I ran off with it.

In the silence that followed I heard Kelly shout, "Get him!"

Someone else yelled, "Which way did he go?"

Then the music came on again. I nearly dropped the speaker unit. Of course! Kelly still had the remote.

I switched it off again and heard them shouting.

"Over there!"

"You two, circle round behind him."

Then the music started again.

I turned the volume down. It took Kelly about ten seconds to work out what I was doing. She turned the sound up to full blast.

On – off – on again.

I kept running, dodging, hiding.

There were twelve of them and one of
me.

The girls were all around me. And they
were closing in.

I'd got no chance, unless – unless I could
take out the batteries! Why didn't I think of
that before?

I fumbled for the catch.

The batteries were out and in my hand.

"Gotcha!" said Kelly as she grabbed me.

Figures rose up out of the darkness.

The church clock began to strike.

The girls stood still, like they'd been turned to stone, as the last stroke of midnight died away.

Then someone giggled.

Someone said, "Nothing happened. Did it?"

"I didn't think it would. Did you?" said another girl.

"Of course not. It was fun though, wasn't it?" said Kelly.

"I suppose so. I'm cold."

"Me too. Let's go home."

I could hear voices coming out of the darkness, drifting off, down the hill.

Kelly and me were the last to go.

When we got back to Nan's bungalow, we didn't climb back in through the window. We used the kitchen door.

Nan was waiting up.

"I was just waiting to lock up," she said.

"Night, Nan," said Kelly.

It was after she'd gone to bed that I noticed the clock.

"Is that the time?" I said to Nan. I checked my watch.

Half past eleven.

"Thanks for reminding me," said Nan. She moved the hands of the clock forward an hour so it showed half past twelve.

"British Summer Time," she said. "It starts tomorrow. Every spring we put the clocks forward an hour. Every autumn we put them back again. Saving daylight, they call it. Silly idea, I call it. How can you save daylight?"

"So it's not really midnight at all?" I said.

"Not for another twenty minutes," said Nan.

"What about the church clock?" I said.

"Mr Frost sees to that," said Nan. "He puts it forward early before he goes to bed."

I couldn't sleep. I sat looking out of my window, waiting for midnight.

The stones were still standing there, up on the hill.

Watching.

Waiting.

I checked my watch. It was almost midnight.

You're not going to believe this, but I know what I heard.

I heard the sound of a fiddle.

You'll say I was still hyped up. You'll say it was a trick of the light.

I know what I saw.

I saw those stones begin to move. Like they were swaying in time to the music, as if they were trying to dance.

Sink the Tirpitz

by
Jim Eldridge

The *Tirpitz* is Germany's best war ship.
Can Bob and the crew of his mini
submarine help sink it? Or will they be
blown up themselves?

You can order *Sink the Tirpitz* from our website at
www.barringtonstoke.co.uk

The Night Runner

by
Alan Combes

Greg wants to win the race. Every night
he trains in secret on the school field. But
he sees a spooky shape in the moon-light.
What is it? Should he run for his life?

You can order *The Night Runner* from our website at
www.barringtonstoke.co.uk

Lucky

by
S. P. Gates

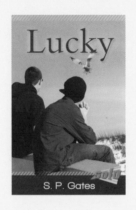

Everyone thinks because Dom is big, he's a bully. But Leon knows what he's really like. And when an injured gull needs their help, Leon finds out there's more to Dom than he thought ...

You can order *Lucky* from our website at
www.barringtonstoke.co.uk

Under Cover of Darkness

by
Pat Thomson

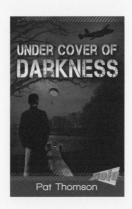

The Nazis have arrived in Michel's village. But the Resistance are fighting back. Can Michel help to win the secret war?

You can order *Under Cover of Darkness* from our website at www.barringtonstoke.co.uk

Cliff Edge

by
Jane A. C. West

Can Danny make the climb of his life to save his friend?
No ropes, no help – no hope?

You can order *Cliff Edge* from our website at
www.barringtonstoke.co.uk